Seymour Greenleaves

Written by

Heather Bowen

Illustrated by

Caleb Peregrine

Three
Quills
Editing

Published by
Three Quills Editing LLC
www.threequillsediting.com

For all the beautiful, unique families everywhere,
and especially for the family I hoped for and was given:
Collin, Sean, and Leia.
You each have my whole heart.
~ Heather

For my littlest sister, Lilianna, so bright and sweet.
I hope that you remember the brotherly love that I have for you,
and I pray that you grow surrounded by
love, friends, and family.
~ Caleb

ISBN paperback: 978-1-963152-00-5
ISBN perfect bound: 978-1-963152-01-2
ISBN hardback: 978-1-963152-03-6
ISBN ebook: 978-1-963152-02-9

Printed in the U.S.A. and U.K.

First printing, November 2023.

Book Cover and Illustrations by Caleb Peregrine.
Book Design by Leia O'Connor and Heather Bowen.

One bright, hot day, a little giraffe named Seymour walked through the grasses of the African savanna. His footsteps were slow and raised tiny puffs of dust, but he walked on, because he was searching for something important. Seymour was searching for *family*.

"We are family," his mama had told him. Afterward, Seymour learned that animal families living on the savanna could not always stay together, even though they wanted to.

But Seymour saw other families while he searched. He passed a monkey mother, snuggling her infant close, and thought of something else his mama had told him. "Family means you are safe."

Later, a mother lion and her cubs rested with sleepy smiles. The sun shone like honey on their fur.

"Family means you are warm," Mama had said. Seymour remembered sleeping beside Mama's warmth on cool nights.

Seymour also remembered his mama's soft, brown eyes, and how she would nuzzle him with her muzzle and say, "Family means you are loved."

Mama had told him something else, too, when the rains stopped, and the savanna grew brittle and bare. "Find a river, Seymour. It will twinkle like tiny stars under the glowing sun."

So Seymour walked, until his legs grew wobbly, and his throat became as dry as the land. When he finally stopped to rest, he spotted something up ahead that shone like starlight. *A river*!

Seymour had never been close to a river before. Mama had fed him milk and all the juicy green leaves she could find, but now it was time for Seymour to drink the river's water.

He walked to the riverbank and bent his long neck. He stretched his purple tongue and tried to drink, but the water was too far away. He crept into the river on little giraffe tiptoes, but he simply could not reach the water.

Then, Seymour saw something floating in the river. It looked like a log, but it had eyes, and they were watching him! Slowly, the something moved through the water . . .

drifting closer . . .

and closer . . .

and closer . . . until . . .

"*Stop!*"

Two animals crashed through the bushes, snorting and stomping!

"Go away, Nile crocodile!" said one of the animals.

"Leave this giraffe calf alone!" said the other.

The animals snorted and stomped until the crocodile turned its head and swam away. Seymour was safe from the crocodile, but he stared with wide eyes at the snorting animals.

"Please don't be afraid!" the first animal said. "The crocodile is gone, dear. My name is Mrs. Greenleaves. Mr. Greenleaves and I are rhinoceroses."

Seymour said, "My name is Seymour. I'm a little giraffe."

"It's nice to meet you, Seymour," said Mrs. Greenleaves, "but where is your family, dear?"

That question made Seymour's tummy ache. He lowered his head and said, "I am searching for family."

"Can we help you somehow?" asked Mr. Greenleaves.

Seymour thought for a bit. "My throat is dry," he said.

"Aah," said Mr. Greenleaves. "The river is safe now. Would you like a drink?"

He made drinking sound easy, but when Seymour tried again, he still could not reach the water.

"Hmm," said Mrs. Greenleaves. "Could you try it like this?" She stepped her legs apart some, then some more, before taking a great, big sip.

Seymour stepped his legs apart, just as Mrs. Greenleaves had done. Then, he bent his neck as far as it would go and stretched his purple tongue all the way down to the clear . . . sparkling . . . WATER!

Slurp, slurp, slurp!
Seymour slurped as much cool, tasty water as his tummy could hold.

He was about to step back from the water, when he saw a face shining up at him. *Family*! he thought. The face looked like the one he remembered, like the face of Mama.

Seymour was so excited, he nearly jumped into the river, but Mr. Greenleaves stopped him, saying, "Little giraffes aren't very good swimmers."

"But I saw *family*!" Seymour said.

"Oh my." Mrs. Greenleaves' voice was quiet. "It was your own face, reflected by the water."

Seymour breathed a big, trembly sigh, but Mrs. Greenleaves told him, "It's a wonderful face, dear."

"Yes, and your eyes are soft and brown," Mr. Greenleaves added. Seymour saw that Mr. and Mrs. Greenleaves had soft, brown eyes as well.

"Your ossicones look very important," said Mrs. Greenleaves, gazing at the two small knobs on Seymour's head. She and Mr. Greenleaves each had two important-looking horns on their faces.

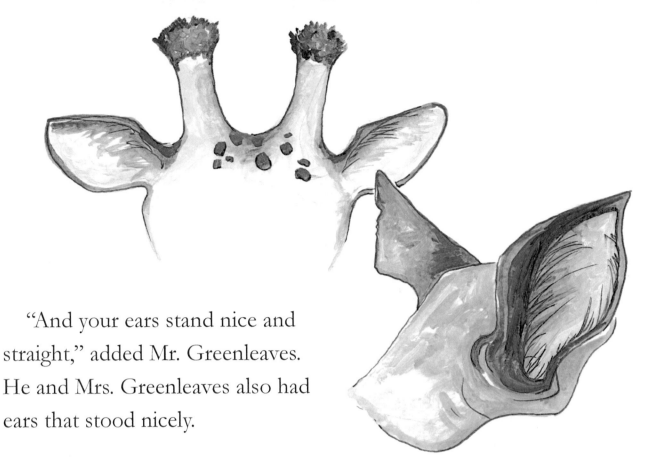

"And your ears stand nice and straight," added Mr. Greenleaves. He and Mrs. Greenleaves also had ears that stood nicely.

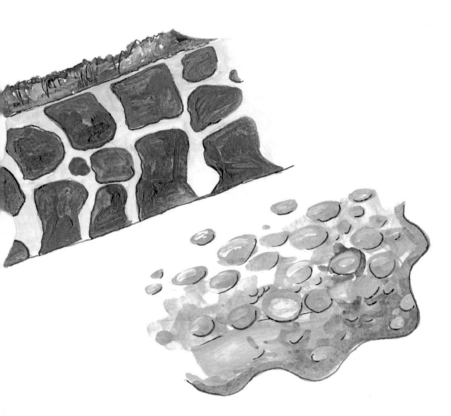

"But I love your patches of color best of all!" finished Mrs. Greenleaves. She and Mr. Greenleaves did not have patches, but they did have strong rhinoceros skin. Seymour thought they must feel very safe inside such lovely skin.

They all stood noticing each other.

Some things were the same and some were different.
That's what made it special.

Before long, Mr. Greenleaves said, "The sun is setting, so it's time for us to leave. The river at night is a place for lions, not giraffes."

Seymour saw the darkness spreading gently over the land. The chill of nighttime was in the air, but he felt warm standing beside Mr. and Mrs. Greenleaves. He also felt safe, especially after thinking about lions.

"Family means you are safe and warm,"
Seymour told the rhinoceros pair. "You
have kept me safe and made me feel warm."

"Family also means you are loved,"
said Mrs. Greenleaves. Her eyes
shone softly, just like Mama's.

Seymour felt a very big question
rise from his tummy.

"Can I be a part of your family?" he asked.

Mr. and Mrs. Greenleaves smiled their widest rhinoceros smiles, and together, they said, "Yes!"

"If you'd like, you can call us *Mama* and *Papa*," added his new rhinoceros mama.

"And we'll call you *Seymour Greenleaves*," finished his new rhinoceros papa.

Seymour smiled his widest giraffe smile. He thought his new name fit him just right, and best of all, when he saw the love shining in his new mama's and papa's eyes, he knew he had found something special. It was just the something he had been searching for.

Seymour had found *family*.

Printed in the USA
CPSIA information can be obtained
at www.ICGtesting.com
LVRC101144060124
768169LV00023B/974

9 781963 152036